D1398448

# Razzle Dazzle

## The Green-Nosed Reindeer

Written by
**Cynthia Ann Powers**

Illustrated by
**Nandi L. Fernandez**

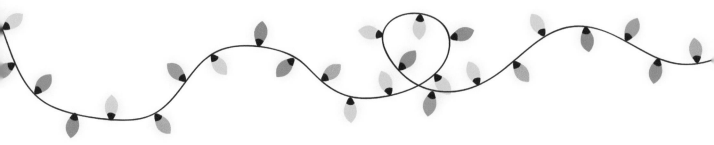

## Dedication

This book is dedicated to my grandchildren -
Brooke, Hudson, Sophia, Quinn and Alexander
- with all my love.

GG

ISBN: 978-0-578-91046-8

## This book belongs to:

_____

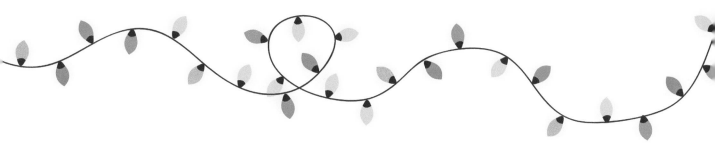

S oft snow fell from a cushion of clouds over the North Pole. Santa Claus was preparing for the Christmas season along with his elves and Mrs. Claus. The workshop was hustling and bustling with saws, hammers and chisels as the elves built the latest toys and games.

The reindeer were practicing their prances and leaps. Rudolph had led them for decades and trained the younger bucks for the opportunity to pull Santa's sleigh full of toys to children all over the world.

Hiding in the pine trees and holly bushes was a young female reindeer named Razzle. She was Rudolph's granddaughter, and she had her own unique nose. It was heart-shaped with a glossy, green glow.

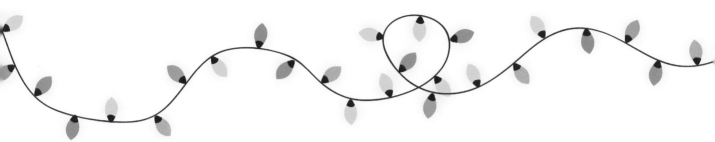

Razzle loved watching her grandfather train the young reindeer, especially Jubilee. He was very agile as he learned to take off, and his leaps were extremely high. Razzle was impressed. She watched carefully and then practiced her own leaps and jumps. She wanted to learn how to fly—even though reindeer girls never flew.

After the training session, Razzle joined her fawn friends playing in the nearby forest. Rosy was always cheery. Posie was calm and still. Carol loved to sing Christmas songs. And Doris was a fanciful dancer who was always tapping her hooves in delightful ways. The girlfriends frolicked in the snow, looking for some fresh nibbling greens.

"What are you so happy about today, Razzle?" asked Rosy.

"Your glee puts a glow on my cheeks," added Carol. "I feel like singing "Joy to the World."

Doris danced with the falling snowflakes as Carol started singing merrily.

"Well, I was watching the young bucks practice learning to fly with my grandfather," said Razzle.

"Ooooh. Was there a special reindeer in particular?" asked Doris, her playful eyes slanting upwards.

"Perhaps," Razzle replied, "And I want to fly too!"

"But only bucks can fly with Santa. Girls never do," added Rosy.

"Why don't we learn?" prodded Razzle. "I want to lead Santa's sleigh someday."

The girls all laughed.

"You wait and see, my friends," Razzle challenged. "I will learn how and I'll be the first girl reindeer to lead Santa's sleigh on Christmas Eve."

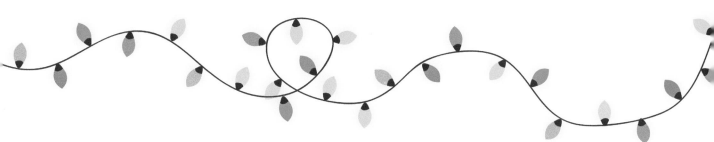

Razzle kicked some powdery snow into the air with her hooves. Instantly, it shimmered and sparkled down, all over Razzle. Her fur was covered in tiny, diamond-shaped snowflakes, like stars illuminating the night sky. Her friends gasped in awe.

Suddenly they heard a rustling sound between the tall fir trees.

"What was that?" asked Doris.

"I don't know," replied Carol, "But look at Razzle."

"Razzle has Dazzle now," said Rosy, "even if girls can't fly."

With that, Razzle turned her back on the others and trotted off, holding her head up high.

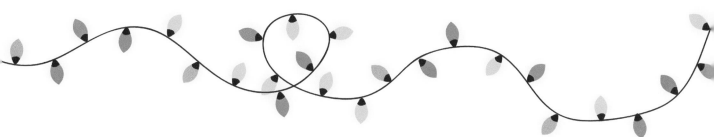

Later that afternoon, Rudolph came into the cave where Razzle lived with her family.

"Why Razzle, you look dazzling," said her grandfather, as he rubbed his nose against her affectionately.

"She came home looking radiant," said her mother, Mara. "We thought it was just snow, but it isn't melting. It's actually getting brighter."

"I was in the woods with my friends, kicked up some snow, and suddenly it sparkled all over me," Razzle explained.

"Christmas magic, I suppose," nodded her father, Nick.

"Maybe it was a visit from the goddess reindeer, Regina?" said Mara.

"Hogwash," Nick argued, sharply. "There's no such thing as a reindeer goddess."

Quickly Razzle changed the subject.

"Grandfather, I want to learn to fly! Will you teach me?" she begged.

Rudolph's bright nose flashed like a red stoplight.

"Razzle, you know girls don't fly."

"Why not?"

"Be…because…" stuttered Rudolph. "They just don't."

"Then you can teach me, Grandfather."

"Stop this nonsense!" Rudolph huffed, then he stormed out.

Tears filled Razzle's eyes. She bolted from the cave and back into the woods.

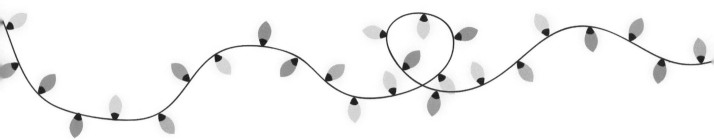

R azzle wandered alone, sighing hopelessly. She longed to fly among the stars.

"Why, oh why can't a reindeer girl fly?" she wondered. She did not understand these silly rules. She looked up into the darkening sky and saw one pulsating star. Was it speaking to her? *You can fly. Just try.* A clear message. Razzle wiped away her tears against a shrub and headed home with new resolve. "I will fly, and no one can stop me," she promised herself.

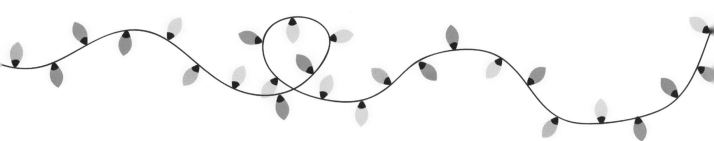

The next day, Razzle went to visit Santa. Surely, now Santa would give her permission to learn how to fly. Rudolph would *have* to teach her.

Santa's snow castle was lined with candy canes with peppermint swirl steps. Gumdrops grew in the trees, as thick as apples. Snowmen swept drifts into igloo-like mounds. Snowflakes floated from the sky in kaleidoscope shapes, delivering wonder and joy. Razzle knocked on Santa's door beneath the holiday wreath. Mrs. Claus answered.

"Well, Razzle, what a delightful surprise! You certainly are glowing and growing into a beautiful reindeer."

"Thank you, Mrs. Claus. May I speak to Santa, please?"

"Of course, come in. He's sitting next to the fireplace reading the children's letters and Christmas wishes."

Santa peered up over his reading glasses and smiled at Razzle.

"Razzle, what a pleasant surprise. How is your grandfather, Rudolph, doing? He must be busy with the bucks," said Santa.

"He is very busy training them."

"Ho, ho, jolly good. Rudolph is still the best."

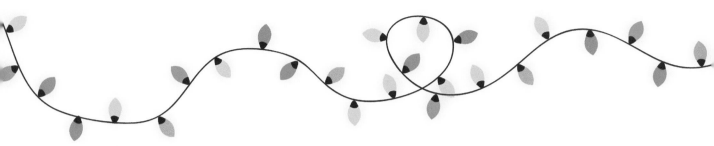

"Yes," agreed Razzle. "Santa ah, ah…I want to train with the bucks and learn to fly."

"What?" asked Santa, removing his glasses. "A girl reindeer… fly?"

"Yes, Santa," answered Razzle, respectfully.

"But girl reindeers never fly."

"Santa, it is time for girls to fly. Please. Will you ask my grandfather to train me?"

Santa rose up from his cozy chair and pulled on his white beard, pensively.

Razzle added, "I don't have a red nose, but my green nose feels and smells where to go and…"

Santa interrupted. "This is highly unusual. It is written in the North Pole laws that only boy reindeer fly."

"Can you write a new law, Santa?" suggested Razzle.

"No, Razzle. I can't."

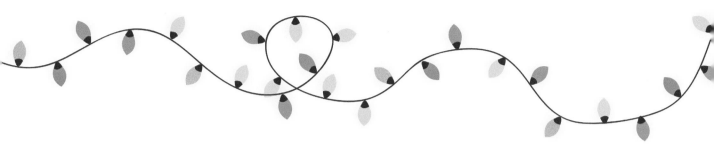

Razzle turned away, blinded by her tears. She stumbled to the door and bumped into Mrs. Claus.

"What's wrong, dear?"

"Santa won't let me learn how to fly. It's not fair." Razzle bolted out of the door into the cold.

Mrs. Claus marched into the living room.

"Why can't Razzle learn to fly?" she asked her husband.

"It's simply not done," replied Santa.

"You can change the law, Santa."

"I can't."

"You mean you won't!" snapped Mrs. Claus. "Razzle is right. Girl reindeer can be taught how to fly."

"Only male reindeer fly!" Santa bellowed.

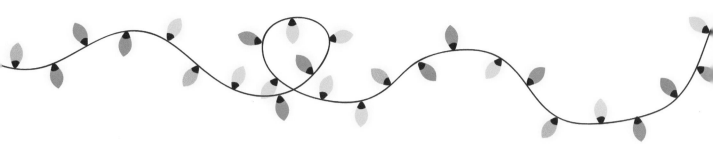

In the shop, the elves could hear Mr. & Mrs. Claus raise their voices. This never happened at the North Pole! Santa was a jolly soul, and Mrs. Claus was a beautiful bundle of joy.

The elves couldn't believe their ears. They hammered and sawed louder than ever to drown out the argument.

Later that day, Rudolph found out about Razzle's visit to Santa. Without wasting a moment, he headed over for a meeting,

"Sorry, Santa, for my granddaughter's behavior. She can be a bit defiant and demanding," Rudolph began.

"Sounds like a great leader to me!" said Mrs. Claus, as she brought in a tray of fresh cookies.

"Mrs. Claus, this is my private conversation with Rudolph. Please leave us alone," said Santa.

"This is my business, too, and Razzle is right," she replied, setting down her tray and straightening her apron. "Why shouldn't girls fly? In fact, now I'm wondering why, in all these years, you never once asked me to join in your sleigh on Christmas Eve. I could help. We could do this together."

"Preposterous!" exclaimed Santa.

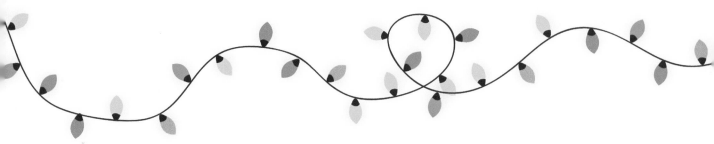

"It's time for a change," stated Mrs. Claus.

Rudolph's blushed and his nose turned extra red.

"I think it's time for me to leave, but thanks for the cookie," said Rudolph, snatching one as he left the room.

Immediately Rudolph went home and scolded Razzle.

"Mr. & Mrs. Claus are fighting, and it's your fault. In all of my years, I've never heard them say a harsh word to each other. It might destroy Christmas."

Razzle fled out of the cave. She was in such a hurry that she lost her footing and fell hard on some ice. A dark shadow reflected on the ice. The north winds whipped and whirled. Razzle was scared. She began to doubt herself.

"What have I done?" she lamented.

"You tried to change things...that's all," said a distant voice

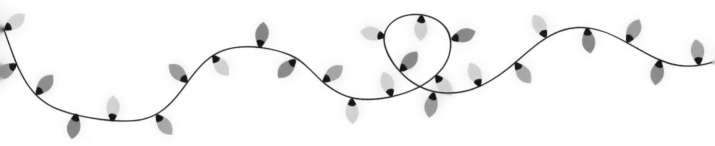

Jubilee stepped out from behind a tree.

"Are you all right, Razzle?" he asked.

"No, I am not all right. I want to be prancing, leaping, and flying like you!"

"So, what's stopping you?"

"My grandfather, mother, father, and even Santa."

"I could teach you," offered Jubilee.

"You would do that?"

"Of course! The first step is to get up. You can't learn how to fly if you are lying in the snow."

Razzle chuckled. Jubilee dipped his head. His small antlers touched hers, and she stood up.

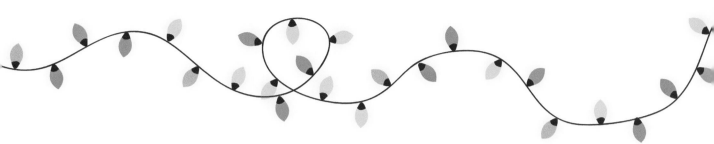

"And you mastered the first step.... getting up on all four legs, " he added. They both giggled together.

Jubilee and Razzle met in secret every day for a week. Razzle felt stronger and stronger, and her leaps more powerful. She had found a loyal friend, and a deep love began to grow between the two reindeer.

Back home, Rudolph was relieved that Razzle wasn't demanding to fly anymore. In fact, her coat looked more radiant than ever.

"It is nice to see you so happy, Razzle."

"Thanks, Grandfather."

"Glad that you gave up on flying."

Razzle tilted her head and remained silent.

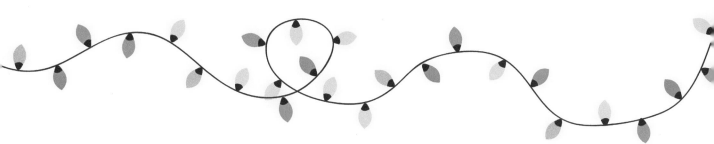

Meanwhile, at Santa's castle, Mr. & Mrs. Claus were hardly speaking. The elves felt sad and toy production slumped. Santa began to lose weight from all the stress. Mrs. Claus stopped baking her Christmas cookies.

The North Pole had started to melt from all of the sadness. The future of Christmas was in serious trouble for the children of the world.

Razzle and Jubilee continued to meet in their secret spot, but the ground was no longer covered in ice —just puddles.

"We need to do something," decided Razzle.

"I agree," answered Jubilee.

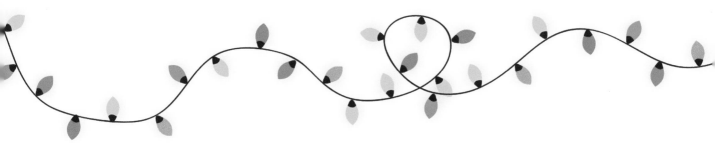

Suddenly a bunch of bucks appeared in the clearing.

"So here you are, Jubilee!" called Strumpet. "We've all been wondering where you've been hiding. Playing reindeer games with Razzle, huh?" Strumpet moved closer to Razzle and poked her with his antler.

Jubilee stepped between them, protecting Razzle. The other male reindeer circled around Razzle and Jubilee. Strumpet poked at Jubilee. Jubilee struck back, and in moments, their antlers were locked in a battle.

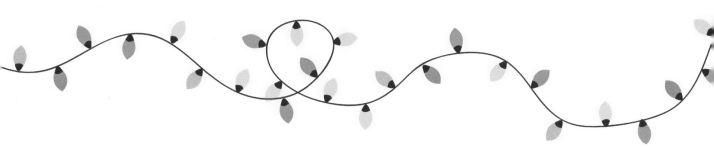

Razzle tried her best to stop the fight, but she got pushed aside by the other bucks. The sky grew black and dark. Suddenly the winds spiraled like small tornados, and the reindeer were blown like flying leaves. They whirled up into the sky. Then fell down to the ground, scattering like fallen branches. They all ran off in fright, except for Strumpet, who squared off with Jubilee and Razzle.

"This isn't over, Jubilee. You got lucky, but I will be the new leader of Santa's sleigh, and Razzle will be mine." Strumpet threatened, then stormed off.

"Are you hurt, Jubilee?" asked Razzle, gently,

"No. We'll just have to find another spot to meet. I refuse to let Strumpet bully me."

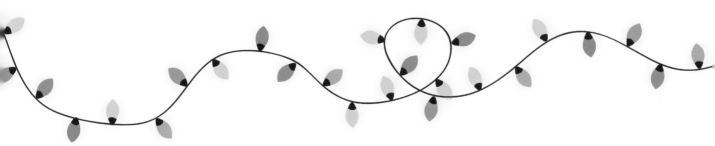

Things got even worse. The North Pole was covered in darkness. Mr. & Mrs. Claus were silent. Toy production stopped.

Strumpet went to the elves. He blamed Razzle for all of their problems.

"Razzle wants to fly and she has caused the entire argument. Can you imagine? A girl reindeer who wants to fly?"

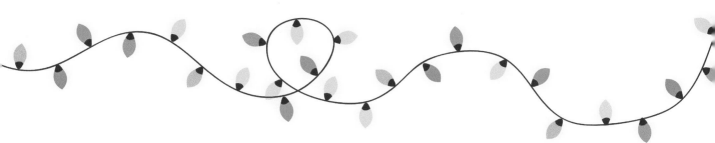

A group of elves gathered and marched off to the cave where Razzle lived with her family.

Rudolph heard them coming and stepped out of the cave to calm them.

"Please, please stop this. My granddaughter is young and only wanted to fulfill her dreams. You can't possibly blame her for everything."

"Jubilee is also to blame," yelled Strumpet. " He's been teaching Razzle how to fly. I saw them together practicing."

"Is this true, Razzle?" Rudolph turned to his granddaughter

"Ah, ah...." stuttered Razzle.

Jubilee stepped out of the crowd and stood near Rudolph and Razzle.

"Yes, this is true. I taught her how to fly."

The crowd gasped.

Rudolph and Jubilee and Nick circled Razzle as the crowd came closer.

Then, as if on cue, a thick fog swirled in, trapping the crowd so no one could see. Razzle, Rudolph, and Jubilee fled the scene, running for their lives.

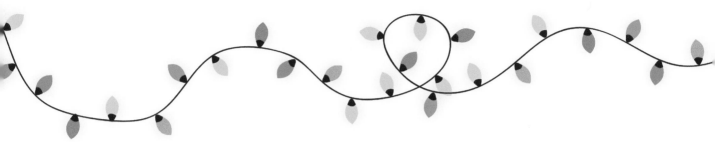

R azzle sobbed. "Did I really do this?"

"Of course not!" insisted Jubilee.

"But they will blame her," said Rudolph sadly.

Then, with a loud crack, the ice beneath them broke and the three reindeer were pulled into a torrent of water. They could barely keep their heads above water. The trio seemed doomed.

Razzle looked up into the sky and silently prayed to the Reindeer Goddess to save all of them.

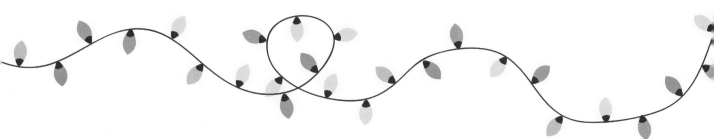

Magically, a star started spinning and shining rainbow colors. Effervescent light reflected on the earth, creating a bridge from the star to the water. Razzle blinked her round, brown eyes in awe.

"Am I dreaming?" she asked herself. "Am I still alive?"

A figure appeared from the star and descended the rainbow bridge. Razzle watched in awe as a beautiful goddess walked towards her. Her hair was ruby gold, and her antlers were high with branches as long as a tree. Beacon balls of multi-colored lights dangled off the branches. Exotic birds with vivid plumage sang in her branches. The sun, the stars and a crescent moon wove between her antlers, and white swirling spirals covered her long, red velvety coat. Sprigs of mistletoe and holly with red berries swayed on top of her tree-of-life crown.

"I am your cosmic mother, and I am here to help you," said the Goddess Regina.

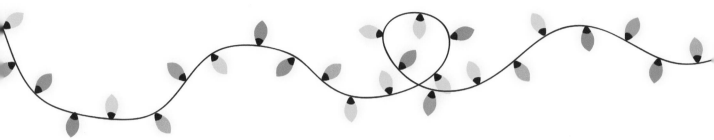

Razzle was speechless. She shook her head nervously.

"You are not dreaming, Razzle. Come, all of you," whispered the Goddess.

The three reindeer levitated out of the water onto the rainbow bridge. Regina beckoned them all to follow her up higher into the sky on the bridge.

"Where are we?" asked Rudolph.

"You are in the realms of the gods and goddesses."

"Are we in heaven?" asked Jubilee.

"Heaven can be anywhere, Jubilee. Your former home *was* heaven, with magic and happiness, but now it is flooding with anger and hopelessness."

"Is it because of me?" pleaded Razzle.

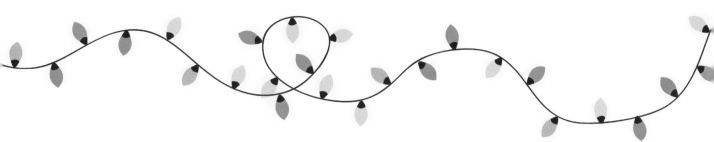

"Yes," answered the Goddess. "But you didn't cause the destruction. It was time for a female reindeer to fly. You had the courage to ask. Jubilee, you had the courage to teach her.

The Goddess paused, choosing her next words carefully. "But Rudolph, for too long, you have kept to an old tradition that needs to change. You, of all reindeer with your red nose, should know what it's like to be different," she scolded.

"You are so right. Razzle, can you ever forgive me?"

"Of course, Grandfather. I love you," said Razzle.

The two reindeer nuzzled their noses together. The soft air surrounding the grandfather and granddaughter filled them with energy and love.

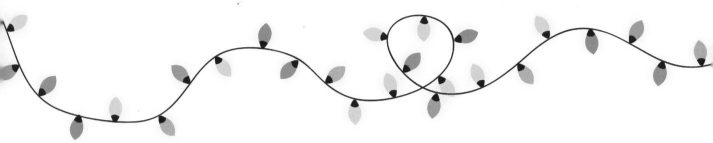

J ubilee," said the Goddess, "Because of your purity, honor and courage, I am bestowing you this great gift."

Regina touched Jubilee's horns, and a spark arched from her antlers to his, changing him into a handsome and pristine white stag.

Rudolph and Razzle gasped.

"Your presence will forever inspire many on earth."

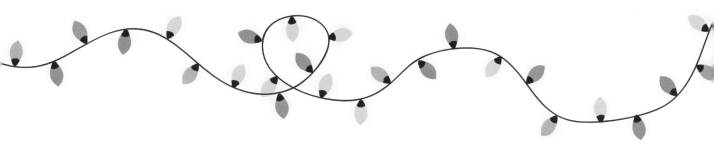

Now, you, Razzle. I have chosen you to lead my sleigh across the night sky on the winter solstice. Earth and its people have forgotten about me, but with you leading my sleigh, I will bring gifts to earth. You will be my single chosen lead. Girl reindeer are all meant to fly. Your dazzling, diamond deer hide will spark magic over the earth."

The Goddess spun like a top, and a royal blue sleigh appeared. Regina flung golden and silver reins over Razzle and hitched her to the sleigh. Razzle's training kicked in as she started to gallop and leap into the sky. She was flying!

They descended towards the earth.

The goddess held a golden cup in her left hand, and she poured amber teardrops. The honey-colored drops rained down and lit a bright light in the hearth of every home.

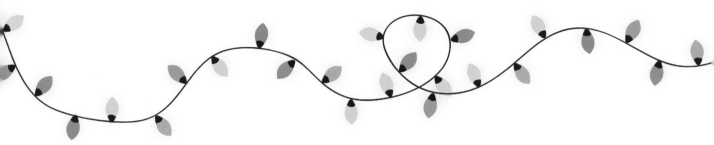

The goddess held a wheel with golden thread in her right hand, and radiant gold leys were woven and weaved around the globe, intersecting and connecting a unified grid of protection around the earth.

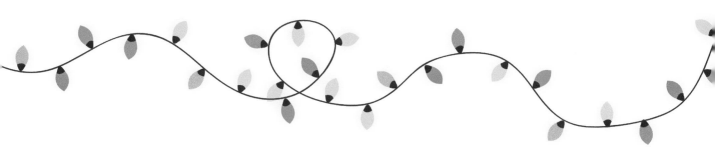

Next, they traveled deeper into the earth. Regina planted seeds of all kinds that would nourish the people of earth. After that was completed, they shot out from the earth's center and flew into the clouds.

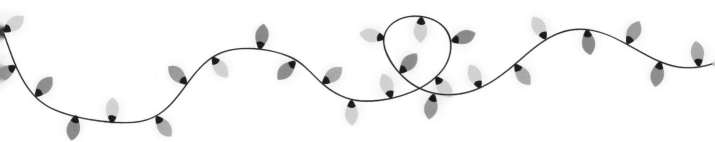

Now, they were over the North Pole. The goddess blew into the clouds, and crystal snowflakes fell. The moment they touched the ground, everything started to freeze back as it once was.

"Razzle," said the goddess, "Sprinkle down your radiance and dazzle everyone with your love."

Razzle shook her coat and radiant rays glistened everywhere.

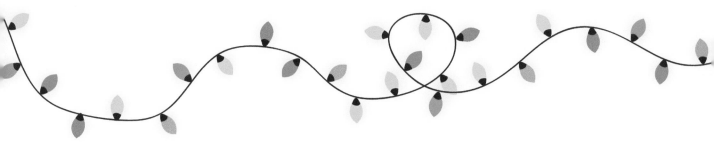

Mr.& Mrs. Claus came out of their house and Mrs. Claus pointed up to the sky.

"Isn't that our dear Razzle with the Goddess?"

"Ho, ho...it looks like her!" answered Santa.

"I knew she could fly!" said Mrs. Claus, clapping happily.

Santa and Mrs. Claus hugged in joy as they saw the magic around them restored.

Razzle soared up higher into the sky as they flew over the rainbow bridge and returned to the lands of the gods and goddesses. Rudolph and Jubilee were waiting, cheering them on.

Regina released Razzle from the sleigh and embraced.

"Now, it's time for all of you to return and share your gifts," Regina said

The trio departed and returned down the rainbow bridge. As their hooves touched the icy ground, the bridge dissolved and disappeared..

Merriment and joy had returned to the North Pole.

Santa addressed all of the elves and the reindeer.

"I hereby decree that Mrs. Claus will be joining me on Christmas Eve to deliver all the toys to the children," he exclaimed.

The crowd cheered with glee.

Santa whistled and shouted, "Next, I hereby decree that girl reindeer will fly as a team with the boy reindeer. Razzle will lead our sleigh with Rudolph."

More cheers and applause.

Then Rudolph stepped forward. "Nothing would please me more, Santa, than to fly side-by-side with Razzle. But I think it is time for me to retire. Jubilee should take my place. Come here, Jubilee."

The crowd gasped as Jubilee stepped forward, his snowy white hide as dazzling as his Razzle as they stood side by side.

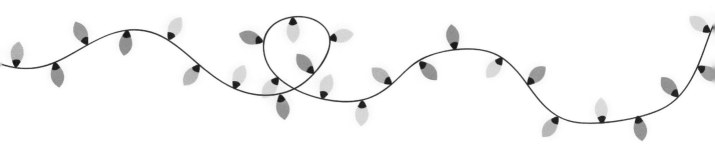

On Christmas Eve, Mr. & Mrs. Claus hopped into their sleigh full of toys. Led by Razzle and Jubilee, the jolly team flew into the sky. Joy and peace were restored to the earth. From that Christmas on, Santa's sleigh always had a girl and boy reindeer leading the way. And every girl reindeer learned how to fly!

## The End

......Have a Razzle Dazzle Christmas!

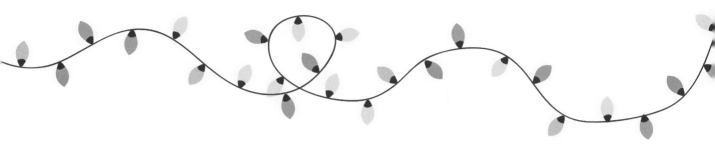

*Author:* Cynthia Powers is a former elementary school teacher who now makes her living as a Shamanic teacher and healer. She is the mother of four adult children - two boys and two girls - and a grandmother (GG) to five. She created *Razzle Dazzle, The Green-Nosed Reindeer* with her granddaughter Sophia while making Christmas cookies. Cynthia believes in the magic of Christmas and the equality of boys and girls. Like Razzle Dazzle.......*she believes in herself & loves to fly!*

*Illustrator:* Nandi L. Fernandez considers herself a global citizen. She is an illustrator, Concept Artist and Animator. A Ugandan born in the United Kingdom, grew up in Uganda, Zambia and Liberia where her love for travel, art and exploring different African cultures was nurtured. Naturally she was drawn to storytelling through visual art, the interest was cultivated during her childhood years having her first published painting at fourteen years old in the Imango Mundi Luciano Benetton Collection.

Graduating high school at fifteen years old, Nandi developed her skills further with a Diploma in Concept Art from Vancouver Animation School and a Bachelors degree in Animation from SAE Dubai. She has since worked as a concept artist at Lionheart Studio in Singapore, illustrates educational materials for the United Nations Children's Fund ( UNICEF) and various children's books while she travels the world.

CPSIA information can be obtained
at www.ICGtesting.com
Printed in the USA
BVHW021827141121
621643BV00007B/315